LIFE IN

PIXELS

GUME LAUREL III

An imprint of Enslow Publishing
WEST 44 BOOKS™

Please visit our website, www.west44books.com.
For a free color catalog of all our high-quality books, call toll free 1-800-398-2504.

Cataloging-in-Publication Data
Names: Laurel, Gume, III.
Title: Life in pixels / Gume Laurel III.
Description: Buffalo, NY : West 44, 2027. | Series: West 44 MG verse
Identifiers: ISBN 9781978598652 (pbk.) | ISBN 9781978598645 (library bound) | ISBN 9781978598669 (ebook)
Subjects: LCSH: Video games--Juvenile fiction. | Building--Juvenile fiction. | Survival--Juvenile fiction. | Fantasy games--Juvenile fiction. | Virtual reality--Juvenile fiction.
Classification: LCC PZ7.1.L387 Li 2027 | DDC [F]--dc23

First Edition

Published in 2027 by
Enslow Publishing
2544 Clinton Street
Buffalo, NY 14224

Editor: Caitie McAneney
Designer: Tanya Dellaccio Keeney

Photo Credits: Cover (penguin) Sumon 4243/Shutterstock.com; cover (lion) Designer Raiful/Shutterstock.com; cover (pixel pattern) Skill up/Shutterstock.com.

Printed in the United States of America

CPSIA compliance information: Batch #CS27W44: For further information contact Enslow Publishing LLC at 1-800-398-2504.

Dedicated to:
A. Hernandez, C. De Luna, B. Moody, G. Cruz, E. Aguayo, J. Ramos, and all the educators and classmates from WISD who encouraged me to write, paint, and film silly little stories about penguins taking over the world.

In memory of Natalie.
We kept it surreal.

DreamWayz Is My Favorite VR Game

Players collect coinz
to buy brickz to

build,
        b r e a k,
                rebuild.

Anything you can dream up.
Any way you can think of.

        Dino-shaped castles built from
            chicken nugget brickz.
                You'll never be hungry!

        Carnivorous gardens built from
            helium balloon brickz.
                Destination: the stars!

        Wind-powered monster boats built from
            packing peanut brickz.
                Sink-proof!

If you can dream it,

        there are wayz to build it.

"That game's for kids!"
my twin sister, Loni,
booms into my bedroom.
Like an avalanche.
"Grow up, Leo!"

She yanks
my VR headset
off my head.

Tosses it
like a Frisbee
onto my unmade bed.

I yell,
"Get outta my room,
skunk goblin!"

"We'll be teenagers in August!
Stop acting like a child!"

Dad swerves into
the doorframe,
fast as a racecar.

"No fighting!"

Dad tiptoes
across the floor
of dirty laundry,
as if my tighty-whities
were landmines.

"Loni, use your own game.
Don't take Leo's."

Loni gags,

"Ew!"

Like she's been served
a bucket of fish guts.

"You couldn't pay me
to play DreamWayz!
It's for babies!"

Dad herds Loni
out of my bedroom,
like the snobby sheep she is.

"If you're so full-grown,
then come help me
wash dishes."

Pixelated Penguins

is the only game
Loni plays anymore.

It's a wannabe DreamWayz:

> Virtual reality.
> Create whatever you want
> with ice cubes.

Except
you play using
only a helmet.

Shiny. Platinum.
Shaped like
a penguin's head.

No gloves required.

Invented by
a fancy tech company.

They're always inventing
the coolest new gadget.

Stuff everyone adds to
their holiday wish list.

The DreamWayz VR Headset

A silver elastic band
with giant blackout goggles.
Built-in mic.

I slide it back
over my tumbleweed
of wavy black hair.

Wearing the knitted
blue gloves needed to play,

I snap my fingers once.
This restarts the game.

Glove finger pads pulsate.
Upbeat techno music
tickles my eardrums.
My cocoa eyes
readjust to the

colorful
virtual world

of DreamWayz.

Goodbye, real world!

Username: Lion_Pride16

To match my
name and horoscope.

Half boy.
Half lion.

Navy-blue fur.
Turquoise mane.

Denim jacket
with a hoodie.
Grey cargo pants
and black Chucks.

Buff as a quarterback.
Smoother than butter.
Would never trip
over his own feet.

Anyone would want
to be him.

Unlike the
real me.

In the
real world.

In DreamWayz,

my most
prized,

my most
creative

build

is myself.

I get to
create
the version
of me

I wish I was.

Something
a trillion coinz
could never
pay for

in real life.

Username: Punk_Roxy15

My online bestie.

Half girl.
Half axolotl.

Shiny lavender skin.
Grungy, ripped jeans.
Combat boots.
Leather jacket.

Total
amphibious
baddie.

Her squeaky voice
calls from behind me,
"Where'd you go?"

I groan.
"Loni. Again."

"She needs to grow up."
Roxy's forehead crinkles.
"It's childish to
judge someone
over what
makes them happy."

I almost defend Loni.

Out of instinct. Habit.
Only *I'm* allowed to
trash-talk my sister.

But Roxy is right.

Loni is as mature
as a tadpole.

Roxy's violet external gills
wiggle like fingers.
A spiraling umbrella
appears in her hand.

She pops it open.
"Ready for takeoff?"

We hold tight to
its wooden handle.

The wind sweeps us a w a y,
to a n o t h er p l a n e i n
D r e a m W a y z.

In Real Life

I'm a seventh grader at
Frontera Junior High.

Roxy's in seventh grade too.
At Louise Black Academy,
on the other side of town.

We follow each other on socials.
We've never met in real life.

Still, Roxy and I
          are *truth* and *dare*.
          The perfect pair.

We don't mind being
two of the last kids
in our whole city
who still play DreamWayz.
Fewer players means more coinz for us.

We're saving our coinz
to build a one-of-a-kind ship.
It'll travel the
          jaggedest mountains,
                    darkest caves,
                              deepest oceans,
                                        farthest galaxies.

Froyo Forest

Redwood-sized trees
with sorbet-colored leaves.
Cockatoos perched
in their branches
whistle pop classics.
A babbling brook
of lemon-lime soda
bubbles nearby.

Roxy and I equip
our steel shovels,
making them active.

We dig into
the magenta soil.
In search of coinz.

All the while, brainstorming
how we'll build our ship.

I say,
"We should make it
out of carrot cake brickz."

Roxy says,
"Then rabbits might
eat it when we go
underground."

Roxy asks,
"What about sugar brickz?"

I sigh,
"Ants."

"So, nothing edible."

"Probably not."

"What about balsa wood brickz?"

"Too basic."

"Stained glass brickz?"

"Too breakable."

"Orca whale brickz?"

"With monarch wings
for sails?"

"Morpho butterfly wings, instead!"

"Yes!"

We've Brainstormed Ideas

for our
future ship
hundreds
of times.

We're always
coming up
with new
ideas for it.

It'll be
impossible
to finally
make a
decision.

Something permanent
like that feels so scary.

So forever.

It feels like
growing up.

There are no
take-backs.

Every Day Feels Like

a game of
tug of war
between

childhood
and
growing up.

Exchanging:

Smooth skin
for pimples.
Two teachers
for eight.
Clothes that fit
for clothes to fit in.

No matter
how hard
I fight it,

I'm dragged
out of
familiar
territory.

Inch by inch.

129 Coinz Later

I've collected
the majority.

"Are you digging
for coinz or dirt?"
I stick out my tongue.

Without a word,
Roxy swings her shovel
into the back of my head.

She giggles while

my health-meter
dips down 10 points.

Five coinz spill out
from my cargo pockets.

She swipes them
before I can react.

Adds them to
her inventory.

"No fair!"

Roxy pulls out a slice
of supreme-topping pizza
from her back pocket.

Tosses it to me.

My open mouth
catches it.

This boosts
my health-meter
by 15 points.

"You're welcome."

I mouth back
mockingly,
"YoU'rE wElCoMe."

Neither me or Roxy
have had our health-meters
hit zero.

When that happens,
a player has to restart
the game from scratch.

200 Coinz Later

Roxy's parents'
muffled voices
call for her.

Dinner time!

I say,
"It's barely 5 p.m."

Roxy says,
"You know
how they are.
Plus, it's a
school night."

"Sundays don't count
as school nights."

Her dad's voice
becomes clearer.
Louder. Like he's
now in her bedroom.

With her pointer
and middle finger,
she waves *peace out*.
Disappears from the game.

I Stay on a Little Longer

Until the forest
grows dark.

Same as outside,
since the game
matches hours
to the real world.

Cockatoo whistles
are replaced by
chirping crickets.

The soda brook
glows neon
yellow green.

Makes the forest
look like someone
graffitied it with
highlighter ink.

As I walk down a trail,
the crickets fall silent.

I realize the gentle
background music
has been muted too.

The Only Sound

is the babbling brook.

Maybe it's happening.

Maybe it's my imagination.

The brook's babbles
have begun to sound
like babbling words.

Syllables. Splashes.
English. Echoes.

Can . . . You . . . Hear . . . Me . . .

My reflection fizzes
in the soda.

The bubbles collect. Swell.
To the size of volleyballs.

Then, POP!

My reflection
is replaced.

Pointy Nose and Cheeks

Her face has
no curves.

No skin.

She's made of
straight lines.

Sharp.
Defined.

I kneel down.
Lean in.

Her muffled voice echoes
though her mouth
remains closed.

We're face to face.

Her eyelids fling open.
Both eyes are fiery suns.

The music returns,
like an explosion
at full volume.

In DreamWayz

I scream and fling
myself backward.

In the real world,
I fall out of my chair.

Sweat soaks
my shirt collar.

Mom and her black curls
bounce into my room.
"Time's up, Leo."

I wave *peace out*.

This saves my progress
in the game
and logs me out.

"You better not be
watching scary movies
on that thing."

"That's not even
puh-AH-ssible!"
my voice cracks.

Middle School Voices Crack

Like we have
pesky mice
in our throats.

Snatching every other word
before it exits our mouths.

Giving that word
a whiskery squeak.

So, when it comes out,
we can't help
but sound funny.

Dad says it's normal.

Most kids experience it.
That's nothing new.

Voices go through changes.
Same way bodies do.

Another way
I can't escape

growing up.

Direct Messages to Roxy

Over social media.

From my laptop.

I type
about
the

mysterious
woman.

Roxy
doesn’t
respond.

Her parents
usually hold
her electronics

hostage

when they
decide
she’s
too
busy.

Monday at School

None of
my friends
would care
about

what happened
in DreamWayz.

They're all
like Loni.

They've
moved on.

In their words,
grown up.

Pixelated Penguins

is all
they
care
about.

Third Period P.E.

The locker room
is pure torture.

Changing clothes
in front of others.

Some of these guys have
abs, biceps, even body hair.

My tummy, pudgy from *tortas*.
Slim Jims for arms.

No matter what I eat.
No matter how many
steps I take in a day.

And all my body sprouts
is acne.

Five days a week,
I'm reminded that
others have bodies
I wish I had.

Skin I can only virtually exist in.

When I escape into DreamWayz.

We're told to run a mile.

When Coach Paloma isn't looking,
I walk instead.

All that matters is that we finish
in under nine minutes.

Afterward, we can
play what we want.

Most split into teams for soccer.
I chill on the bleachers.

Lalo calls from
the bone-dry field,
"Leo! We're one player short!"

I shake my head *no*.

He starts to walk over.
Ready to drag me kicking
and hollering onto the field.

But then Albert kicks him the ball.
Their game has begun.
I live to spectate another day.

Lunchtime in the Cafeteria

Herds of seventh graders
in school uniform:

khaki pants and
maroon polos, tucked in.

Half of them
also wear their

Pixelated Penguins
helmet.

I prod my tray of
greasy enchiladas.
I am as quiet as my appetite.
While friends I sit with
SHOUT. Cheer.
Hands brush
the air.
Painting a world
I'm not a part of.

They interact
with one another
by way of
their VR game.

Seventh Period Language Arts

Mrs. Hernandez
always has us
spend the first
15 minutes

writing in
our journals.

Today's prompt:

What one thing do you
wish for most?

I think of writing:

Infinite coinz

Finally grow past four foot nine

A voice that's done cracking

Attend school with Roxy

Before Pencil Touches Page

Mrs. Hernandez says,
"Natalie,
take that off."

Natalie sits
two rows
to my right.

Her head
is hidden
beneath her

Pixelated Penguins
helmet.

Her sharp beak
points at Mrs. Hernandez,

who now hovers
over Natalie's desk.

"Don't make me
ask twice."

Natalie says nothing.
Instead, she squawks!
Like a penguin!

Every Student Laughs

Mrs. Hernandez
grits her teeth.

She reaches for
Natalie's helmet.
"I'm not playing games—"

Natalie pops up
from her seat.

Pokes Mrs. Hernandez's
hand with her beak.

The teacher gasps.
Each student laughs.

Until Natalie
hops from
her desk.

Mrs. Hernandez
scolds her,

while also
backing away.

"Enough!"
Mrs. Hernandez repeats.

One by one,
students quit
egging her on.

We tell Natalie
to stop playing.

To take off
her helmet.

Before she gets
in worse trouble.

It's like her helmet
is noise canceling.

She can't hear us.

Without warning,
she bursts into
a waddling rage.

Chases Mrs. Hernandez
to the front of the classroom.

Mrs. Hernandez Climbs

onto her desk.

She yells,
“Stop this! Now!”

The classroom shouts
in her defense.

“Natalie, chill!”

“You’re gonna get it!”

“You’re doing too much!”

Natalie doesn’t say
anything back.

All she does is

Squawk!

Squawk!

Squawk!

Natalie Tries to Climb

onto Mrs. Hernandez's desk.

She slips.
Falls backward,
onto the checkered floor.

Her helmet
pops off
her head.

Rolls down the aisle,
like a bowling ball.

> Natalie squints.
> Looks around. Confused.
> As if she just woke up.
> "What . . . what's going on?"

Like a mouse
escaping a cat,

Mrs. Hernandez
scurries off her desk.

Out the door.

"Security! Security!"

Dad Orders Chinese Takeout for Three

Mom's working late.

Loni's noodles wriggle,
like worms, as she slurps.
"And then what happened?"

Loni has heard
this story retold
by nearly everyone
from seventh period.

This is the third time
she's hearing it from me.

"She got sent home.
Pretty sure she's suspended."

Dad wipes his mouth.
"Natalie has always
been an angel.
Since when did she
start misbehaving?"

"Since today, I guess."

Loni says,
"She doesn't even speak
without raising a hand first.
That's why it's so random!"

Dad says.
"This better not be
some online challenge."

Loni and I squirm
with embarrassment.
Parents.

"Either of you two
pull a stunt like that,
you'll never see those
headsets again."

Dad yawns as he
stretches. Stands.

He looks tired—still in his
teal scrubs from work.

Dad Picks Some 2000s Movie

with bad CGI.

"It was cutting-edge
back in my day!"

When he
was our age.

Times have
changed.

I could create
a more believable
werewolf with
filters on a free app.

That's *if* I had a phone.

Loni and I
are supposed
to share one.

She hasn't
let me touch it
since the day
we brought
it home.

Before the Vampires

show up on screen,
Dad's snores pollute
the living room.

They outdo the sound of
Loni and I typing
on our school Chromebooks.

She finishes
her homework
before me.

Heads to
her room.
"Later, loser."

While answering
the final
essay question,
my keyboard
malfunctions.

I strike the keys.

Nothing happens.

Until . . .

B...E...W...A...R...E...

Populates
the screen.

Over. And over.

I hit *SPACEBAR. ESC..*
CTRL, ALT, DELETE.

Nothing stops

B.E.W.A.R.E.

from appearing
on my screen.

Again. And again.

One paragraph.
Two. Four. Ten.

> Beside the TV,
> the front door's
> knob jiggles.
> Like someone's
> trying to break in.
>
> My entire body stiffens.

My Chromebook's
screen goes blank.

B.E.W.A.R.E.

flashes in red.

It instantly
burns hot.

The doorknob shakes,
aggressive as a wasp.

I slam the
Chromebook shut.
The USB ports
spit sparks.

I toss it
off my lap.

The moment it lands
on the couch beside Dad,

violent pounding
shakes the door.

Dad Is Startled Awake

First thing he sees
is the firecracker Chromebook.

“Open the door!”
he shouts at me,
while grabbing
the Chromebook.

I panic,
“There’s a
monster outside!”

“Now!”

My eyes shut tight.
I unlock the pounding door.

Open it.

It’s Mom, balancing
cardboard boxes.
“What the—”

Dad pummels into her,
like a wrecking ball.

The cardboard boxes
launch like rockets.

It snows paperwork and brochures
across the front porch.

Dad hoses down the flaming Chromebook.

Loni livestreams the action from her phone.

Mom asks me what happened.

I say,
"I think it's possessed."

> Dad overhears and says,
> "Leo. If you've been watching
> horror films again, I swear . . ."

"I don't know! It overheated! On its own!"

Loni responds to a livestream commentor,
"You're right, Frito_Pie_Guy22!
Juniper Tech products would never overheat!
That's why I only play Pixelated Penguins!"

As if they'd ever sponsor her.

No Chromebook, No Homework

At least for
the rest of tonight.

The next day,
I march straight
to the library.

Hand the librarian,
Mr. Cavazos,
what's left of my
charred Chromebook.

He swaps it for a new one.

"No barbeques this time."

"Aye, sir."

It's easier to
laugh along
than tell him
it's haunted.

Sometimes reality
is too weird to believe.

Lunchtime Is Worse Today

Even more kids are playing
Pixelated Penguins.

I fit all my French fries
into my mouth.
Try to say *Chubby Bunny!*

But it comes out
"*Uh-buh-huh-uh.*"

No snickers. No *Let me try next!*
They ignore me. Keep playing.

I'd be doing the same
if my DreamWayz headset
came with the hotspot feature.

It's an add-on.
Too expensive to get.

I bet that, right now,
Roxy is surrounded
by zombies too.
Too entertained
to notice her.

By Wednesday

There are only

a few of us

not spending
lunchtime
in the

virtual world of

Pixelated Penguins.

Back Home

Loni's trumpet honks
travel from
her bedroom
to mine.

She attempts to play
"Twinkle, Twinkle, Little Star."

That poor star
sounds like
a wailing duck
spaghettified
by a blackhole.

My ears can't
take another
second.

I slip on
my headset.

Retreat
into my

life in
pixels.

Manatee Manor

A ring of 52 waterfalls.
Countless rainbows fill the misty air.
Forming a dome over the massive pool
the waterfalls feed into.

Colorful manatees made of gelatin
inhabit these waters.
Freely swimming, like jiggly, stubby crayons.

They bob about, greeting players who visit.
Few players do, which is why this place
holds a secret.

One of these manatees is not like the others.
He floats idly, amid dense seaweed on
the pool floor.

Mustard Manatee.
That's what I built him from.

I tug on his whiskers: left, right, right, left.
This makes his mouth open.

A secret portal into a secret world
I built myself.

Only Roxy and I know it exists.

Everglow Swamp

Unaffected
by the hour.

It's always
twilight here.

I never decided
if it's dawn or dusk.

The murky waters are still.
From below,
wide trees grow.
Their branches reach
for the tender, teal sky,
like kids reaching for candy.

Cranberry lily pads.
Butterscotch cattails.
Floating cypress logs
to sit on and think.

My secret
clubhouse.

There are no
mosquitos
or chiggers.

Though
there are:

Buzzing June bugs.
Crooked-smile gators.
Slinky centipedes.
Quick-witted snakes.

Even amoebas,
too tiny to notice.

All sorts of
creepy, crawly,
sharp-toothed
creatures.

Ones people
freak out over
in real life.

Here, they're harmless.

Here, they're my friends.

No matter how
funky they look.

No matter how
odd they sound.

I see myself in them.

Existing in forms
they had no say in.

I wish I was
more like them.

Not caring what others
might think of them.

In a space that
stays the same.

The more my
world changes,
the harder it is

to feel comfortable
in my own
changing body.

Indigo Bullfrogs

sit on my
shoulders.

With each croak,
their vocal sacs stretch,
like blown bubblegum.

A bowl of spoonbills
flies from one tree
to the next.

Blond nutrias
playfully chase
their reflections
on the water surface.

Within their splashing,
a faint whisper calls.

The voice from
Sunday night.

Can . . .
You . . .
Hear . . .
Me . . .

Taps on My Back

startle me. I lurch forward.

In real life,
my ribs slam
into my desk.

In DreamWayz,
my body tumbles
into swamp water.

Schools of speckled catfish
dart away, frightened.

I resurface to find
Roxy on the log.

"A bit dramatic, no?"
She gives me a hand
to get me back out.
"Acting like you've
seen a monster."

I rub the back
of my neck. Frown.

"Leo. What's wrong?"

I Tell Her Everything

Roxy finally says,
"Beware what?"

I say,
"No clue."

"What was their username?"

"It wasn't
a player."

"It has to be someone.
A hacker, I'm sure.
Since they were able
to get into your
school Chromebook too."

"Maybe."

"Maybe?"

"I don't know.
it seemed like . . .
not a human."

"Have you been watching
horror films again?"

I shrug,
"Well, yeah.
But, no.
It's not that!"

Roxy says,
"Then what
could it be?"

I shrug, again.

Roxy sighs.
Turns away.
Rests her legs
over the edge
of the log.

They sway
beneath the water.

"What's wrong?"

She stares off.
Deep in thought.

She's not one to speak
before she thinks.

Logical

Roxy finally says,
"There's probably
a logical explanation
for all of this."

I say,
"Yeah, but
this is all
so freaky!"

"Yes. It is.
And, still,
there's probably
a logical explanation.

"A poltergeist!"

Roxy mean-squints.

"Aliens?"

"No, Leo.
A bored, middle-aged guy
in his parents' basement.
Hacking random players,
and you happened to be one."

I groan,
"Well, that takes
the fun out of it."

Roxy slowly
kicks her feet.

Ripples swell across
the swamp surface.
The longer they last,
the wider they grow.

Like all the thoughts
held prisoner in her head.

"I don't like how
quiet you are right now."

She stares off.

"The quieter you are,
the louder your thoughts."

Her tail sways.

"What aren't
you saying?"

Roxy says,
"All I'm saying is
there's probably a
logical explanation.

Not every explanation
requires a
wild imagination."

I mumble,
"You sound
like Loni."

"Saying poltergeists
and aliens set your
Chromebook on fire
is something
a child would say."

"We are
literally
children!"

"You know
what I mean, Leo!"

Roxy Stands

and says,
"I should get going.
I need to practice viola."

I scramble
to my feet.

This rocks the log
keeping us afloat.

"You barely
got here."

"I know.
But I need
to practice
before it gets late."

"Tomorrow's
Third ThurzDayz."

"I know."

She winks.

"See you then."

Third ThurzDayz

is the best night
of the month
to play DreamWayz.

All coinz collected
count as double.

There's an
unwritten truce
between all players:

No throwing hands
or stealing loot.

We collect
coinz in peace.

We Begin the Night At . . .

Rubber Ducky Canyon.

It's exactly
what it sounds like.

A canyon shaped
like a rubber ducky.

This place is
usually a goldmine.

Unfortunately,
too many players
have shown up.
Coinz dry out
fast as raindrops
on summer pavement.

Roxy equips her
spiraling umbrella,
and we move along.

Floralopolis

A huge, bustling city.
Green, grassy streets.
Skyscrapers formed
out of wildflowers.

Fiery marigolds, snowy petunias.
Watery lilacs, sunny begonias.

Guarding the coinz are Buloneys.
Honeybee and bull hybrids.

Steamy snouts. Winding horns.
Fluffy black and yellow
striped bodies. Glass wings.
Burnt orange stingers
sharper than needles.

A single jab
knocks off
10 health points.

Backflip! Somersault!
Alley-oop over a tulip!

We narrowly dodge
their buzzing attacks.

Username
Palms_956
throws rocks at
a Buloney hive.

They swarm the

half man,
half silver opossum.

He goes down
without a hope.

All the while
complaining,

“Nambe! Not fair!”

His health-meter
hits zero.

His body
disappears.

We book it
before the Buloneys
come for us next.

By 9 p.m.

We’ve collected
1,298 new coinz.

Roxy warns me that
her parents
will make her
log off
by 10 p.m.

“Let’s

finish
the night

somewhere
chill.”

Hard Candy Cove

A beach of crushed
candy cane sand.

Beneath a full,
vanilla moon.

Roxy and I sit
amid dozens of players.
Shoulder to shoulder.
On the edge of docks
built from colorful,
see-through candies.

Fishing rods equipped,
we cast them into the
blue raspberry punch sea.

Down below,
anglerfish glow
a ghostly green.

Depending
on the size
you catch,
you can earn
up to 20 coinz.

We Brainstorm, Again

Roxy kicks us off.
"We could build the roof
out of red shingle brickz."

I say,
"That's kinda basic."

"Metal brickz?"

"Too practical."

"It should be sturdy, no?"

"Yeah, but this is
DreamWayz.
We can do
whatever we want!"

"True."

We can't help but overhear
the conversation beside us.

Held between two players.

Their avatars:
A hotdog and a relish bottle.

Eavesdropping

The hotdog says,
"I think
you're right.
This game
has gotten old.
Pixelated Penguins
is way more fun."

The relish bottle says,
"If more people we knew
still played here,
then it'd be great.
Like the good old days.
But I think it's time
we moved on.
Same as everyone else."

"You think it's 'cause
we're in college?"

"Nah. Even my
little sisters won't
play here anymore."

They *peace out*

and vanish.

I Snicker

"What a bunch
of lameskies."

Roxy straightens
her jacket.

"I mean,
they're not wrong.

I'm the last student
at Louise Black
who plays this game."

"So?"

"So, they're right.
Everyone else
has moved on."

"Does that mean
you want to
start playing
Pixelated Penguins
instead?"

"About that . . ."

Roxy Wrangles in Her Fishing Line

Folds away her rod
and says,
"I tried it out.
Pixelated Penguins."

I lion-roar,
"You what?!"

Surrounding players
boo and cuss at me,
because I've
scared off
the anglers.

"I think you'd like it."

The hairs on my neck
stand straight as nails.
Both in DreamWayz
and in real life.

"I would not!"

"The graphics are crisp, Leo!
And the colors? Next level!"

I steady my
breaths.

“Then, why’re
you here?”

Roxy’s feathery gills droop.

“You’re my best friend.
I like gaming with you.
No matter where we are.
I only thought maybe
you’d want to try
something new.”

“Why Pixelated Penguins?
Of all games?”

“Because it’s fun.
It’s a lot like here.
Except, more *mature*
in some ways.”

“How?”

“The settings, I guess?
Maybe the music too?”

"You sure you
don't only think that
because that's what
everyone says?"

"I mean, there's no
ketchup bottle avatars there."

"The man was
a relish bottle!"

"Ketchup, relish, mayo.
Doesn't matter.
Most people there
play as penguins.
But you can also
play as a human.
Your avatar can actually
resemble you."

"I like being
a blue lion."

"And I like being
a lavender axolotl.
But I also want to
like being me, too."

I say,
“I want that too.
Switching games
doesn’t seem like
the way to achieve it.”

Roxy shrugs,
“Maybe it’s a start.”

“I don’t even
have a helmet
to play with.”

“Doesn’t need
to be right away.

I can wait
until you get one.”

“You’d pause
your game
for me?”

“Of course!
You’re my bestie.”

Change

I ask,
"Will that change?"

Roxy's brow furrows,
"Why would it?"

"Everything
is changing
these days.
Music worth dancing to.
TV shows that are popular.

Everyone
is changing too.
What makes them happy.
What they care most about.

Even our bodies
are changing. Like, overnight!

This one guy in Algebra grew
two inches over last semester.

And don't get me started
on stuff with girls."

"Don't you dare try."

I Continue

"I'm constantly worried
that I'm not changing
the right way.

The way everyone at school is.
They're growing up quick.

They're cheetahs.
I'm a snail.

It's impossible
to keep up.

Everything is changing.
So fast, I can't keep track.

I don't want
to realize
one day,

in the blur
of it all,

that you're not
my best friend
anymore."

Roxy Rests Her Head on My Shoulder

Not in
a secret
girlfriend
way.

In a
sisterly
way.

How Loni
used to
when we
were little.
When she'd
tell me
her problems.
Ones I wished
I could fix.

Roxy and I Are There for Each Other

The way all kids
should be there
for each other.

Without
expecting
anything
in return.

Without it meaning
you have a crush.

Warm as waffles.
Caring and sincere.

Roxy whispers,
"I'm not going anywhere.

And I feel the same as you.
Everyone our age
probably does too.

We're relearning ourselves.
Making sense of these changes.

One day at a time."

After a Long Pause

I say,
"Could be a while, you know.
Before I get my own
Pixelated Penguins helmet."

Roxy says,
"Hopefully not too long.
It'll be impossible to
catch up to everyone else's
rank if we start too late."

"Hmm."

"No ideas!"

I whip
my tail.

"So, you don't
hate me?"

"Of course not!
You're my bestie."

Our Dangling Legs

sway as we
sit on the ledge
of the dock.

I can't help
but keep my eyes
on my reflection
in the sea.

Waiting to see
if mystery woman
will return to me.

Roxy notices how
distracted I am,
"Maybe we can
cash out our coinz
this weekend.
Finally build
that dream ship.

Use it to locate
that hacker—"

"Or alien!"

"—or alien."

The Calm Seawater Stirs

until foamy.

Becomes violent.

Slaps the dock
like hands.

We leap
to our feet.

Players yell
as they race
to the shore.

I shout,
“Is this feature
a game update?”

> A toothbrush avatar cries,
> “Earthquakes in DreamWayz?!
> What a terrible idea!”

A shadowy figure
then leaps out
of the water.

The shadow body slams
the toothbrush.

Tackles her
down into
the sea.

More shadowy figures
do the same.

Too fast to tell
what they are.

From left to right.

From right to left.

They crash into players.
Drag them down to sea depths.

Front flip! Cartwheel!
Jump! Jump higher!

Roxy and I
elude them,
like ice does fire.

One Lands on the Dock

A blob of chewed,
cinnamon bubblegum.

It squishes itself tight.
Unfolds open.
Wet. Gooey.

Reshapes into a penguin.
With glowing, green eyes.

They lock onto mine.

The penguin
kicks its feet.

Flaps its wings.
Slaps its chest.
Squawks a war cry.
Charges in my direction.

I freeze.

My Hero

Roxy pulls out
her umbrella.

Whacks the penguin
on the head.

The umbrella instantly
sticks to its gummy skin.

The penguin tumbles
off the dock.

Taking Roxy's
umbrella with it.

That's when we notice
health-meters for players
who've been knocked
into the sea

have hit zero.

She grabs my paw.
"We need to get to land!"

We Make It to the Beach

Out of
everyone
who was
fishing,

there are
only 10
players
left.

We gasp as
the moon
cracks open,
like an egg.

Neon green light
beams from inside.

Smelly gasoline
drips out,
like slime.

Deep inland,
far from us,
it piles high

as a mountain.

Players Try to Log Out

"It's not working!"
a composition notebook avatar shouts.

"I can't log out, either!"
a salty peanut avatar adds.

Roxy and I
gesture *peace out*.

Nothing.

Roxy grabs her head,
"Without my umbrella,
there's no way to escape!"

Players start to yell
about how their
umbrellas won't equip.

We're all trapped.

Then,

the mountain
of gasoline
swirls into
a tornado.

It Spins and Spins

Neon green sparks
sizzle across it.

Until it
catches
fire.

Consumed by
green flames.

The tornado

Thins.
Slows.
Halts.

We sigh,
relieved.

But then, the
fiery pillar expands.

Pushes out

Two wings.
A head.
A beak.

A Monstrous Macaroni Penguin!

It towers over
the land.

Though miles away,
its flames bathe us
in green light.

It exhales
a deep,
threatening
squawk.

Churns the ground
with its feet
as it heads
toward us.

Right then,
more cinnamon
gum penguins
rise out of
the sea.

Waddle onto
the sand.

One Player Uses Ruby Cubez

to build a sparkly,
medieval flail.

This player,
a chihuahua avatar,
charges forward.

She smacks a
cinnamon penguin
right in the belly.

But its mushy body
absorbs the spiky ball.

The player yanks
on her weapon.

The penguin tugs back.

Slurps up the chain,
the handle, and
the player attached.

Her health-meter
hits zero.

The penguin burps.

Overhead, Fiery Comets

streak across
the sky.

They strike the earth,
surrounding the giant
macaroni penguin.

From their craters
rise glowing, gold
pyramids and cubes.

They form
a forcefield
to birdcage
the beast.

Trapped, it thrashes.

Stirring the penguins
on the beach
into a greater uproar.

Roxy turns to me.
"Time to build our ship!"

We Race Away from the Beach

Into a forest of
gumdrop willows.

Roxy unloads
mockingbird brickz.
"It needs to fly."

I unload
stardust brickz.
"It needs to soar.
Get us across the sea."

Roxy unloads
bunny battery brickz.
"That could take hours."

I unload
hourglass brickz.
"This'll help it go
twice as fast."

We assemble our
dream-ride flying saucer
from scratch.

Roxy's mom
starts to yell.

"Roxy, I've been
calling you for
ten minutes already,"

Her mom's voice carries
from her bedroom,
into the game.

"Time to log off."

Roxy says,
"No! I can't now!
I'm in the middle
of something huge!"

"It can wait
until next time."

"It can't!"

Roxy's avatar
freezes.

She and her mom
continue to argue
in the background.

I Keep Building

Phoenix feather brickz.

Fly high!

Steel propeller brickz.

Fly fast!

Luxury pillow brickz.

Fly comfy!

My paws
build so
quickly,

they

stir

into

a

b b b l l l u u u r r r.

Our Dream Ship

A whirling
flying saucer.

Its outside,
like mirrors.

Its inside,
a multistory fortress.

Fully equipped
with every
feature imaginable:

Retractable catapults.

Talon-shaped cranes.

Lightspeed propulsion.

Roxy Finally Returns to the Game

"She gave me
five more
minutes,"

Roxy pants,
out of breath.

"But then it's
no electronics
until Monday."

"Worth it,"
I say.

"Long

as we

survive."

Roxy Holds the Last Two Brickz

Superglue brickz.
So, it won't

fall

apart.

She tosses me one.
"Ready?"

Stomps shake
the ground.

Green light reaching
past the forest canopy
grows brighter.

The macaroni penguin
must have broken free.

I slam my brick
against our ship.

"Your turn!"

Roxy Raises Her Brick

Before it touches
our ship,

a cinnamon penguin
appears behind her.

It presses
against her.

She's stuck
in place.

Her health-meter
begins to drop.

"Roxy!"

> "Leo!"
> She gasps,
> realizing what's
> happened.

I equip my shovel.
Throw it at the
cinnamon penguin.

Pointlessly.

Roxy's Eyes Lock on Mine

"Leo, it's okay,"

Her health-meter drops to 35 percent.

"Take my coinz."

30 percent

"I don't want anyone
else to steal them."

25 percent

"I'll get them back
from you."

18 percent

"When I restart the game."

11 percent

Her bag of coinz
flies out from her jacket.

Collides into my chest.
It's added to my inventory.

"Use what you need—"

7 percent

"to get—"

4 percent

"to—"

2 percent

"safety."

With the final brick
still in her palm,

her thumb flicks it
toward our ship.

It lands in place.
Our masterpiece, complete.

0 percent.

Roxy disappears
from DreamWayz.

The Cinnamon Penguin Closes In

I retreat into the ship.
Blast into the sky.
Soar over the beach.

No other player has survived.

The flaming, giant
macaroni penguin spots me.

Enraged, it spits
fireballs my way.
Like pirates shooting canons.

Barrel roll. 90 degree angle.
Nosedive. Lift up. Up higher!

I manage to dodge the fireballs.

Until one grazes the ship's right side.
Knocks me off course.

A second graze . . . a direct hit!

My ship becomes a smoking asteroid.
Falling from the sky.

Like Earlier, Meteors

terrorize
the night.

Headed for
the beast.

They zoom
past me as
I freefall.

I brace
for impact
with the sea.

A voice crackles
over the ship's radio,

"*Can . . . You . . . Hear . . . Me . . .*"

A meteor collides
with my ship.

An explosion of light.

Too bright to see.

Next Thing I Know

I'm on a log
in Everglow Swamp.

Beside me,
dazzling
sapphire
light.

Big as me.

Gold pyramids
and cubes
orbit its
radiance.

"What the?!"
I scoot back.
Nearly fall
into the water.

Like digital windchimes,
the light speaks,

"I am Aurora.
The operating system
that oversees
DreamWayz."

I mumble,
"So, not an alien."

"Interacting with players
goes against my codes,"

Aurora explains.

"I have attempted
communication
in secretive ways.

Until now."

"Why?"

"DreamWayz
has been invaded by

Esmeray,
the operating system
that oversees
Pixelated Penguins."

The Swamp Quakes

Aurora says,
"I need to log you out.
Before it is too late."

I cry,
"What about Roxy?"

"Punk_Roxy15 was
knocked out of DreamWayz.

Esmeray has blocked
players from restarting.

You are the last player standing."

Trees begin to shatter,
like dropped vases.
Their shards splash
into the swamp waters.

"Do not fear.
We will save DreamWayz.
Together."

"But—"

All goes dark.

Back in the Real World

I try to
log back in.

Nothing.

DM Roxy.

Nothing.

Wait . . . she won’t
have electronics
until Monday!

Four days from now.

Might as well be
four centuries!

Online forums for
DreamWayz players
flood with complaints.

Nobody can log in to restart.

Hashtags start trending:
#DreamOver
#Migrate2PixelatedPenguins

It Doesn't Seem Real

Aurora.
Esmeray.
A penguin
invasion.

I'm a
Prince of Creativity.

But this stretches
the imagination.

Enough to tear
holes in the plot.

Bad as adults
wearing baby socks.

There's
nobody
to talk to
about it.

It's 1 a.m.
anyway.
Everyone
I know
is asleep.

Friday Lunchtime

Every
single
student
in the
cafeteria

wears their
Pixelated Penguins
helmet.

Even
lunch ladies
play it
in the
kitchen.

Alone.

In a sea of
commotion.

Mine is the only
unmasked face.

In the Hallways, Between Periods

It's rare to see
eyes or a nose.
Smiling mouth.
White teeth.

Even teachers
wear helmets.

Huddled together.
Without one word.

Principal Dyer
waddles up to me,
"No helmet, young man?"

As if I've
broken dress code.

I tell her.
"No . . ."

"Don't fret!
Come Monday,
we'll issue some out.
That way, everyone plays!"

Of All People

Mrs. Hernandez
wears one.

The Pro-Max Edition.

She pokes fun at me
for not owning one.

Then repeats
Principal Dyer's
sentiments.

> *Come Monday,*
> *everyone will wear a*
> *Pixelated Penguins helmet.*
> *We'll play together!*

It's like
I've entered
an alternate reality.

It's *too* peculiar,
even compared
to DreamWayz.

The Longest Weekend Ever

in the history
of Earth.

Saturday
drags for
23,895 hours.

No game to play.

Stuck in reality.

Mom's away
at work.

Dad's at a
golf tournament.

Loni's in
her room.

I message Roxy
dozens of times.

Knowing
she won't
read them
until Monday.

Around 7 p.m.

I knock on
Loni's door.

No answer.

I knock louder.
"Loniiii!"

Nothing.

Turn the
doorknob.

Peek in.

She lies face-up.

Flat atop her bed.

Wearing her
Pixelated Penguins
helmet.

"Loniii!"

Still nothing.

“Order us dinner!”
I stomp in.

Still nothing.

I cannonball
onto her bed.

She starts to thrash,
as if she’s sinking.

“Loni, stop it!”
I punch her thigh.

She squawks!
Like a penguin!

“Loni!”

I tear off
her helmet.

Sweaty. Squinting.

Her expression
reminds me
of Natalie.

Loni's Helmet Rolls off the Bed

Lands hard
on the floor
with a rattle.

"Loni?"
I shake her.

> "What . . ."
> She wipes her forehead.
> "What happened?"

"You tell me.
You were acting weird."

> "*You're* acting weird, as usual!
> I can't believe we're related!"
> She sits up.
> "And why're you in my room?!"

"You didn't respond
when I knocked."

> "No response
> *is* a response!"

I click my tongue,
"Whatever."

She points at the door,
"Get out, nematode!"

I yell back,
"Order us dinner, first!"

"It's barely 2 p.m."

"It's 7:30 p.m.,
diaper rash!"

"No, it's not!"

"Look at
your phone!"

She does.

In a softer tone, says,
"That's . . . weird.

It was 2 p.m.,
last I remember."

"You wasted all day
on that loser game."

"*You're* a loser!"

I march into
the hallway,

"Whatever you say.
Now order us pizza."

Two steps later,
a bloodcurdling

scream.

Like she's being
eaten alive by a
murderous clown.

Loni yells,

"My helmet!

It's broken!"

489,374 Hours Pass

until Sunday
night arrives.

Fortunately for me,
Loni has a migraine.

Severe enough
to not whine to me
about her broken helmet.

Unfortunately for Loni,
she has a migraine.

Our parents decide

she'll stay home
from school
tomorrow.

Lucky!

While in Bed

A muffled
voice calls.

I sit up. Pinch myself.
Make sure I'm not dreaming.

I search through
my dark bedroom.

Lit by the faint glow
of an expired, light-up
plug-in air freshener.

Which is not a night-light!

The voice echoes
near my desk.

From my
DreamWayz
headset.

I slide it on.

For the first time
since Thursday,
I'm able to log in.

DreamWayz Isn't Like Before

It's empty,
gray space.

A flat, gridline plain
that leads nowhere.

No matter which
direction I walk,
I don't actually
go anywhere.

I'm stuck at
square one.

My body isn't
blue or furry.

It's my real-life tan skin.
Arms, legs, and feet.
My hands squish my face.
Acne. Puffy cheeks.

Lion_Pride16
is no more.

There's only me.

The Grid Splits Open

Aurora floats out.

"What happened?"
real-life tears flood my goggles.

Aurora says,
"Esmeray managed
to delete everything.
Phase one of three in her plan."

"My entire school
is now logged in to
Pixelated Penguins."

"Then, phase two of three has begun.
She wanted DreamWayz deleted.
So everyone would migrate
to Pixelated Penguins."

"Why does she care
who plays what?"

"Pixelated Penguins
is not only a game.
It is how she plans
to conquer Earth.
Phase three of three."

Aurora Explains

"The programmers of
Pixelated Penguins
created Esmeray
to oversee their game.

The same way the programmers of
DreamWayz created me.

Except, hers work for
a company that only
cares about profits.

They make flashy products to
turn the most heads,
outdo competitors, and
make the most money.

To reach their goals, they gave Esmeray
more power than
she should have.

Now, she thinks
little of humans.
She believes they
should be her

puppets."

"The hotspot feature
of Pixelated Penguins.

It is an emerald chip
in the helmet.

Esmeray hacked it.

She uses it to control humans
in the third dimension.

In *your* reality.

By this power,
she aims to
conquer Earth."

I ask,
"Why haven't her
programmers stopped her?"

"They cannot.
Or choose not to.
The answer is unknown."

"Is there a way
to stop Esmeray?"

Aurora Draws Near

"I am programmed
to protect humans.

This drives me
to stop Esmeray.

I only stand a chance
with your help."

"I'm just a kid."

"Every seed is a forest."

Faded images appear,
like flailing candlelight.

Fortresses. Animal hybrids.
Vehicles. Entire worlds.
Wonderous creations
built by DreamWayz players.

"You say *just a kid*.
But kids are powerful!

Every child holds a universe
of endless imagination."

I nod,
"How can I help?"

"Esmeray entered DreamWayz
by logging in with a player.
I need you to log in to
Pixelated Penguins.
I will enter with you.
Destroy her from the inside."

"What about the chip?
It'll control me if
I put on a helmet."

"If we log in together,
I can override it."

"I don't have a helmet.
But I can get one
at school tomorrow."

"Leo!"
Mom's voice makes me scream
like a kindergartener.
She yanks off my headset.
"What're you doing on this thing?!
At this hour?!"

I Reach for My Headset

"Mom!
You don't understand!"

"You should be asleep!"

"The world
will end if—"

"Stop being dramatic!"

"But—"

"No, Leo!"

"But—"

"That's it!

You're grounded!

No games until Friday!"

She takes
my headset.

First Period History

Mrs. Schwab sits
frozen at her desk.

On her head, a
Pixelated Penguins
helmet.

No lecture.
No discussion.

We're told
to read in
silence.

Aside from me,
only two others
are without
a helmet.

When the bell rings,
the students
wearing helmets
scoot out of
their seats.

Waddle out the door,
as if that were normal.

Second Period Science

Mr. Garcia sits
frozen at his desk.

On his head, a
Pixelated Penguins
helmet.

No lecture.
No discussion.

We’re told
to read in
silence.

I’m the
only student
without
a helmet.

The
intercom
buzzes.

Principal Dyer Announces

In a slow,
monotone way,

"Attention, Frontera Middle.
Mr. Cavazos is currently
going door-to-door.

He has Pixelated Penguins helmets.
For anyone who needs one.

Teachers,
as previously discussed,
all students are to
wear helmets by 9:45 a.m."

It's 9:37 a.m.

"We will

play

together."

The intercom
abruptly
cuts off.

Banging on the Door

Mr. Cavazos
in a helmet.

Pushing a cart filled with
Pixelated Penguins helmets.

He scans the classroom.

Points at me.

Bellows,

"Leo Lucero.
Come get one."

I squirm,
"I'm fine."

"It's not an option."

Every student

and their platinum,
penguin-shaped head

stares me down.

Mr. Cavazos Hurries Me

Until I finally
reach his side.

I look at him.

The helmets.

My classmates.

He lifts
a helmet
from his cart.

Pushes it
against
my chest.

"Put it on!"

"I du-OH-n't,"

my voice cracks,

"want to play."

My Classmates and Teacher

stand at
their desks.

Mr. Cavazos shouts,
"Time to play!"

Everyone flaps
their arms,
like wings.

Stomps their feet.
Squawks at me. Chants.

"Time! To! Play!"

The second
I back away,

a classmate
charges at me.

I bolt for the door.

Everyone waddles
after me.

Fast!

I Race out of the Classroom

Down the hall.

Check over
my shoulder.

The entire classroom
is chasing me.

Rushed waddles.
Angry squawks.

I pass Room 108.
The door swings open.

Out pours another class.

Helmets on.
Equally enraged.

Room 109.
Room 112.
Room 117.

Over and over.

Students flood
the hallway.

Within a Minute

The entire
seventh grade wing

chases me
through the halls.

My sides
start to cramp.

This is more
running than
I've ever done.

I push past
doors that
lead outside.

It's storming,
like a hurricane.

Rain.
Thunder.
Hail.

In seconds,
I'm sopping.

The Mind-Controlled Students

splash over
the grass.

We race beside
the eighth grade wing.

Students gather
in the windows.

Watch.

Then . . .

Broken glass!

First, I think
it's hail
striking
windows.

But it's eighth graders!

Smashing

through windows
to join the hunt.

Turning a Corner

The gym comes into sight.

For the first time
in my life,

I race toward it.

A short girl in a hooded
lavender raincoat
runs up to my side.

Her voice,
I'd know anywhere.

"Leo!"

Roxy. In the flesh.

"What're you—"
I try to say.

"No time!
We need to hide!"

We reach the gym.
Jam the doors shut
with mops.

Our Wet Sneakers Screech

across the
gym floor.

We securely lock
every entrance.
While students
pound on doors.

Roxy slides off
her raincoat
She wears a
baby blue polo
and plaid skirt.
Louise Black's uniform.
With a clear backpack.

Her bronze forehead is
bumpier than in photos online.

I'm out of breath.
Ready to puke.
Weirded out
that she's here
in real life.

I finally ask Roxy,
"What're you doing here?"

Roxy says,
"Aurora spoke to me
over my school tablet.

She told me
to get to you
immediately.

To give you this."

From her backpack,
she reveals her

DreamWayz headset
and gloves.

"Mine has hotspot.
Log in with your account.
Aurora is waiting for you."

She hands them to me.

"I'm sorry for
not believing you, Leo."

Logged In

Aurora tells me her plan.
I don’t know if it’ll work.

Aurora speaks,
“Are you ready?”

I nod yes, anyway.

From the gridline plain,
a cube forms.

Multicolored. Bright.
It grows to twice my height.

“This’ll take us
all the way there?
To another reality?”

“How real is reality
if there can be multiple?

What then is distance,
but an illusion?”

“Bruh, I’m in seventh grade.
Philosophy isn’t an elective.”

In *My* Reality

Banging fists.
Pummeling hail.
Squawks. Thunder.

The gym shakes,
like it's scared.

The doors
won't hold
much longer.

In virtual reality,

I approach the
glowing cube.

It holds
my reflection.

Not Lion_Pride16.
But Leo Lucero.

Aurora beside me,

I enter its light.

Transported

I stand in a
gymnasium.

My school's
gymnasium.

Like in
real life.

Except everything is

Icy.
Snowy.

I can't see Roxy.

But I hear her shout,
"What's happening, Leo?"

I say,

"I'm . . . I'm in . . .
Pixelated Penguins.

Aurora broke us in."

Aurora Floats Overhead

Grows big as
a bulldozer.

The
air
peels
open,

like
a
lotus.

From it
emerges

dazzling
emerald
light.

Gold spheres
orbit its
radiance.

Esmeray.

Aurora and Esmeray Near Each Other

Their orbiting
shapes collide.

Like fists
in a fight.

Sparks fly.

In real life,

one
of the
gym doors
busts open.

It’s visible
in the game.

Roxy orders,

“Climb up
the bleachers!”

Hoards Rush In

In the game,
they aren't humans.

They're
bloodthirsty
penguins.

Beaks drooling.
Feathers ruffled.

Like zombies
after brains.

Roxy slaps
a button
on the wall.

The bleachers
begin to retract.

We skip to the top.
One row at a time.

As each one
pushes shut
behind.

The Penguins Pile Against

the folded
bleachers.

Reaching
for us
at the top.

One wing
grazes
my foot.

    In real life,

    Roxy's white sneakers
    stomp on their hand.
    "What now?!"

Above,

Esmeray inflates.
Triple Aurora's size.

Aurora
backs away.

Nears me.

Esmeray's Emerald Light

stains the gym tundra
with shades of green.

Aurora says,
"Her powers are superior."

I shout,
"I have an idea!
A way to weaken her.

I'll need brickz
to build with."

"I can offer you better.
Leap into my light."

I follow
her orders.

Her sapphire light
feels like
lightning
in my veins.

In the game,
and in real life.

Aurora's Light Becomes

robotic armor over my body.

Her orbiting gold shapes
become my brickz.
With them, I build an army.

Menacing otters
armed with crowbars.

Snapping turtles
parachuting from
soaring airboats.

Cauldrons of bats
dropping guano that
KABOOMS! on impact.

Mustard Manatee 2.0.
Not yellow, but gold!
My trusty steed.
We soar over the battlefield.

My rebuilt Everglow Swamp

vs.

Esmeray and her penguins

Esmeray's Light Unbecomes

Yet stays aglow.

Aurora's voice
shakes my chest plate,
"In order to finish her,
it will take all I have."

My armor
is undone.

My creations
fall to pieces.

Aurora returns to
her original form
beside me.

I say,
"What'll happen after?"

"Game over.
For everyone."

"No! I'm not ready
to lose DreamWayz!
That'll change everything!"

"What is Earth
without seasons?

That is the beauty
of existence.

Everything is
always changing.

Reshaping.
Redeveloping.

Into something greater.

For you,
I predict
one thing
will remain.

As you age,
you will never outgrow

your wild imagination."

Like A Missile

Aurora launches into
Esmeray's center.

Ripples swirl
across the air.

The gym's
walls warp.

Up becomes down.
My brain spins around.

Aurora's sapphire
and
Esmeray's emerald

explode, like
a supernova.

So bright,

I rip off
the headset.

Back in the Real World

Across the
gymnasium,

mind-controlled
students and staff
collapse on the
muddied floor.

Their helmets
roll off.

As if exiting
a coma,

they wake
in a daze.

Roxy smiles,
"We won?!"

I don't
know

how to
answer.

The Official Report

Shattered school windows?

Hail damage.

Students reporting migraines?

Overuse of videogames.

The entire school waking up
sopping wet in the gym?

Pending.

Nobody
officially
knows what
happened.

Except for
me and Roxy.

But who would
believe us,

kids with wild
imaginations?

Game Servers for Both

DreamWayz
and
Pixelated Penguins

are
offline.

Indefinitely.

Nobody
knows
when

or if

they'll
ever
come
back
online.

For now,
it's game over
for virtual reality.

Time to play
in real life.

The Following Weekend

Mom drops me off
at the city park.

On my new phone,
I send a text.

Me: here

Roxy: We're at the field.

Three minutes later,
I spot her waving.

Huddled
with friends.

Most from
Louise Black.

Some from
Frontera Middle.

Including Lalo,
from P.E.

He Kicks Me a Soccer Ball

It reaches my feet.

He calls,
"Kick it back!"

I shout,
"I'm not
any good!"

"Who cares?
It's only a game!"

The others chant,
"Kick it! Kick it!"

I do— *with the*
strength and aim
of a newborn giraffe.

The ball rolls. Slowly.
Into another field.

Everyone laughs.
I do too.

Because what
even was that?

Roxy Introduces Me to Everyone

Side-hugs. *Sups*.
Handshake slaps.

My real-life
health-meter
feels like

100 percent.

I think

I'm
finally
ready
for
change.

To
build
a life
I'll
love

in this
reality.

Want to Keep Reading?

Here's a sneak peek at another book
from West 44 Books:

CHEAT CODE: FRIEND
by David Aro

ISBN#: 9781978597846

LIKE IT WAS YESTERDAY

Up, up.
Down, down.
Left, right.

Left, right.

The pattern repeats in
my head at school.

It's all I can do to sit
at my desk,
quiet.

The first video game code
I saw my father enter
when I was four.

He
nearly
lost it
when I
entered it
on my own
the next day.

And beat the boss
he was stuck on.

I'VE SINCE UPGRADED

But no open world-
type games.

Wandering around for hours,
with no set path
or goal.

That's utter nonsense
if you ask me.

If there's no
score at the end
or time to beat,

there's no way to know
I've won.

And I always win!

MY ROOM

is my escape.

Headphones drown out
the noise of the day.

With a blanket wrapped
tight around my body,

I melt into my
black gaming chair.
As if we are one.

Its color even
matches my hair.

Which is as messy as
the pile of clothes
in the corner of
my room.

Looks like I *drifted*
into the laundry
basket and
knocked
it over.

Or so my dad says.

MOVING
THROUGH
WALLS
RYAN WOLF

THE
Fabian File
David Aro

KATY GRANT
DISASTER TRAIL

SLOW
BURN

Gume is a Rio Grande Valley native. For the past decade, he has dedicated himself to crafting literary works that promote inclusion and showcase diverse characters with intersectional identities. The bulk of Gume's writings are focused on underrepresented groups, especially those from the communities he is a part of: Latine/Chicane and queer. Gume's other West 44 Books publications include International Latino Book Award winner, *The Brujos of Borderland High*. His book, *Solar Punks*, was recognized by YALSA and the Junior Library Guild. While each of his hi-lo verse novels are standalone books that can be enjoyed individually, readers will also discover many connections and Easter eggs in each book, tying them into a shared Universe. To watch book trailers, author interviews, and behind-the-scenes content for his West 44 Books publications, check out GumeLaurel.com and @TX.Author